A Noisy End & Other Short Stories

Ritaban Biswas

ISBN 978-93-5458-575-3

Published in India 2021 by Pencil

A brand of
One Point Six Technologies Pvt. Ltd.
123, Building J2, Shram Seva Premises,
Wadala Truck Terminal, Wadala (E)
Mumbai 400037, Maharashtra, INDIA
E connect@thepencilapp.com
W www.thepencilapp.com

DISCLAIMER: *This is a work of fiction. Names, characters, places, events and incidents are the products of the author's imagination. The opinions expressed in this book do not seek to reflect the views of the Publisher.*

Author biography

Ritaban Biswas is an undergraduate engineer with a penchant for reading and writing poetry & short stories. He's been in the world of storytelling since he could remember. *ANoisyEnd& OtherShortStories*is his debut book. Currently, he lives in Kolkata, West Bengal, India.

CONTENTS

A Noisy End

"Gotta get up, gotta get out, gotta get home before the morning comes/

What if I'm late, gotta big date, gotta get home before the sun comes up."

Everybody despised Jay's favourite pair of headphones and wanted to hide it, somewhere undiscoverable, for his good- but in vain. No one has ever seen him without that devil, not in daylight, at least, as if his resilient ears breathed through it. The more pesky side of the story was that he played the same song on loop. Thus, "Jay was addicted" would be an understatement, for what was he addicted to? The tuneful Gotta Get Up? The pair of blue and baggy headphones? The singer? It could be anything.

"Did you talk to Jay about his headphones? He's getting out of hand now-" asked Mira, the conscious mother of Jay, to her husband, at the dinner table in their son's absence.

"Okay, how about 'he doesn't listen to me'?" retorted Jagdish, the noblest man anyone around him has ever come across.

"C'mon Jagdish, you're his father! Moreover, he loves you more than me and listens to you too. You know that, right?"

"I know you're worried, Mira. But it is, kind of, normal for teenagers. Also, when I was his age, I listened to Elvis Presley as much as I could!"

After a few moments of tranquillity, Mira rebuked, "Why aren't you bothered at all!"

"Okay-okay, calm down, woman! I'll talk-"

"You'd better before it's too late."

Post dinner, Jagdish went to the terrace, the only place to find Jay on sombre nights. He was standing at a corner with his headphones tucked in, probably playing the same track.

"Could we talk, Jay?"

He didn't reply.

"Jay," this time a bit aggressively, " just put off that song-" he stopped, realising that Jay won't be able to hear him out. However, he could sense his father standing behind him. Removing the sloppy devil, Jay turned around and uttered," Did you say something?". Jagdish tried to keep his feelings to himself and didn't want to handle the situation with anger. "How was your day at school?" "Monotonous, as usual. Why do you ask-" Impatience grew in Jagdish, and he got straight to the point.

"What's so addictive about this song anyway? Y'know, you could damage those weary eardrums if you listen to any kind of music for unusually long hours."

Jay didn't reply; instead, he didn't care to answer. He went to his room- the most uncanny departure ever. He was drowsy but didn't want to sleep. The surreal music called for him as if it needed Jay's ears to sustain. He kept the headphones on the side table beside the bed and, before switching off the lights, he glanced at them. It was gleaming in the strangest hue of azure as if beckoning him over. However, he managed to restrain himself and, switching off the lights, went to bed.

Saturdays have always been lively in Bhubaneshwar- every living being gets more lively, with the heart prancing in high spirits. The clock struck seven. Jay never required an alarm to wake up. This day wasn't an exception, except that he woke up with a sudden jolt. Unlike every morning, Jay couldn't hear the mallards' morning calls. All he could hear was Harry Nilsson, singing his favourite track. Neither did he tuck in his headphones, nor would anyone barely play it at that time of the day. It was just ringing in his ears and playing in his brain. He liked the weird situation he was in that he had always wanted to live in. Nevertheless, he was weirded out and tried finding out the source of the music but couldn't. Ignoring the seriousness of the situation, he got back to business.

In the beginning, he could at least listen to one of his parents reprimanding him for not listening to them. But gradually, all he could do was perceive them murmuring.

Finally, he reached a stage where he could hear nothing but the loud track.

An hour passed.

"Gotta get up, gotta get out, gotta get home before the morning comes/

What if I'm late, gotta big date, gotta get home before the sun comes up."

Jay finished his breakfast without having to hear his parents and went to his room. He sat morbidly on his bed, left undecided of his next step. How could he go out without being able to hear anything, not even the cars honking, except a track that was eating up his brain? On the other hand, his thinking capacity was shrouded by the music- it was turning onerous for him to think or even talk to himself. He couldn't feel anything, for every time he tried to, the music showed up. It seemed as if the song ran through every vein, artery, and organ in his body that debarred him from feeling anything save numbness. He decisively got up on shaky feet, went at the open window, looked down, and tried listening to the daily clamour of the neighbours, their kids, the passers-by, and the cars. But, he failed to. He was about to burst into tears, but the numbness of emotions didn't allow him to tear up. He remembered his parents' warnings against listening to music for long hours, especially his dad's last words to him the previous night.

"What did you tell Jay last night that he's ignoring both of us?"

"I don't understand this boy anymore, Mira. He's hell-bent on not leaving his headphones and that damn track!"

"Okay, wait. We are in this together. How about now? C'mon, let's go to his room."

Both Jagdish and Mira went to Jay's room, which was locked from inside. They knocked on the door simultaneously- their son didn't answer it. "My goodness! He's again got himself on the damn pair of headphones- watch me throw it away in front of him!" shrieked an angry Mira. Jagdish knocked vigorously but to no avail. "Break it!" screamed Mira, with an air of sudden alertness. After heavily pushing against the door a couple of times, it broke open and fell to the ground.

The sinister headphones, still gleaming, were lying on the ground beside Jagdish's feet, splintered into more than two pieces. However, one of the pieces was stuck into one of Jay's ears, whose blood-smeared corpse was resting on the ground.

The Photo

Jen was too tired to drag herself to the bedroom. Her feisty boss and shrewd colleagues bring the worst out of her- there's no detachable moment to breathe at the workplace. Living in solitude since joining *Panache*has been a bane for her- she has to do every chore by herself. Moreover, she sees difficulty in trusting anyone, implying that she's a housekeeper as well.

Her bedroom wall clock struck nine o'clock, and she was vexed to remember that she hadn't cooked that day. The worst miser to have ever existed, she would never order food online. With growing hunger pangs, a sullen Jen prepared for bed. Suddenly, her boss called.

"Did you forget something?" enquired Mrs Samantha, with an air of sarcasm.

A moment of silence prevailed while Jen rigorously asked herself, and she remembered after that.

"Y-yes, Samantha- I mean "No", I didn't. I'll be sending the photos to you as soon as"

"I need those photos from the meeting right now. Don't make me regret counting on you." Samantha hung up.

Jen wanted to know why and how her life had turned upside down. The meetings are the worst- she has to see every face, ready to trap her in a scornful air- the meeting!- she had almost forgotten what was to be done; she cursed everyone.

Before her cellphone dies, she has to send the photos featuring her rude, yet plump and fair, boss- just like Miranda Prie from "The Devil Wears Prada". Jen rummaged in her phone's gallery until she came across something quite unnatural, given her lifestyle: a photo of herself in a lie-down shot probably at night. Jen was tired but not in a state that her brain would go berserk in interpreting stuff. Forgetting what she had to do, she was transfixed by the photo- "-is this me?". Well, there were other important questions like, "-who took the photo?" or "-where are Samantha's photos-"; but the latter was redundant then. The savvy millennial that she is, Jenna swiped up to know the details of the photo- it was clicked on 20/20/20, at 20:20. But, does a date like that even exist? Moreover, it's still March, and there are, like, 12 months in a year- she questioned herself repeatedly, and the more she did, the more perplexed she became. Now, she scrutinised the photo-

"-do I see anyone else?- No."

"Maybe, a shadow- Not one except mine."

"All I need is a clue-"; Jen could decipher nothing that could take her to the truth.

She had wasted a quarter of her time in the strange photo of her, and Mrs Samantha's deal flew off her mind. About time. She was called again. In terror and disgust, she answered it.

"Glad you answered it. I was about to declare you dead-" Samantha said calmly.

"Oh- actually, something eerie has happened to me-" Jen blurted.

"Are the photos safe?" asked Samantha, with the most sarcastic tone ever.

In almost a plight of crying, Jen replied, "I'll be sending them to you in a while." and hung up.

Momentarily, something eerier occurred- she couldn't see her photo anymore! She tried finding it by date, which would never exist! She was more bewildered than terrified- "-was it a mistake out of delirium?", "-had I been dreaming all this while?"; she didn't have an answer to any of these.

Remembering Samantha and her photos, Jen found them and sent them to her. She assumed that her brain wasn't working at pace, which made her see the picture earlier that night. In self-satisfaction, she lied down to sleep and let her friend, the brain, rest for at least 20 hours.

Lost & Found

Rudy was an otherwise patient man, but he wondered what could take Nat, his sixteen-year-old son, fifteen-odd minutes to buy a couple of insignificant groceries. He was seated comfortably on the driver's seat; eventually, he got out for some air and tried sneaking into the shop but backed away and decided to wait. While Rudy's anxiety was about to skyrocket, he saw Nat coming out of the store with the items he was asked to buy. However, he seemed sketchy.

"What took you so long, Nat?" asked Rudy politely.

Momentarily, Rudy realised through Nat's bubbly eyes that something weird had happened to him. He wasn't terrified but didn't seem alright either.

After a dramatic pause post his father's question, Nat replied, "I think I saw someone."

"Someone- who?"

"Mom."

Instantaneously, Rudy reminisced how his wife, Mindy, was run over by a six-wheeler on their sixth marriage anniversary while she lagged crossing the road. Since then, he remembers her every night and imagines how their lives would have been better had she been alive. In a jiff, Rudy was brought back to the present by a truck, revving nearby.

With moist eyes and anger, Rudy's voice cracked while he replied, "I didn't expect you to bring this up as a joke-"

"Why would I joke about it in broad daylight, dad? I truly saw her with my sober eyes! Moreover, I'd approached her, but she seemed to have left the shop from the other door- I just stood there, reminiscing-"

"Get in the car.", rebuked a distraught Rudy.

Knowing he wouldn't be believed, Nat acted accordingly. Rudy drove themselves straight home without uttering a word. Up there, he was blank; he looked at his son, who glinted at every human they crossed by. He didn't want to scold him- he'd never wanted to. Since Mindy's untimely demise, Rudy has pampered their son as much as a father could so he won't miss his loving mother. And that wasn't going to alter for a mere joke, as he thought.

Rudy drove hastily, which took them ten minutes to reach home. As soon as they entered, Nat sprinted to his room. At that moment, Rudy wished he could believe his son and check for his wife- his dead wife- in the adjacent alley. All these seemed imbecilic to Rudy, even though he was mawkish. He told himself that he was overthinking and buying the words of a kid. But then, he wished they were true.

The grandfather's clock, which was almost as old as Rudy, was about to strike nine. Since they returned home, Rudy hasn't heard a word from Nat. He'd also refrained from visiting his son in his room, who generally keeps himself busy with books and sports. It was dinner-time. After being called twice, Nat didn't get out of the room, which began worrying Rudy. After the third call, he decisively went upstairs.

The door to Nat's room was slightly open. As Rudy peeked, he saw his son looking at the starlit night sky- a reflective, sad young man.

"What's the matter, big guy? Aren't you hungry?"

Nat turned towards his father and replied with an unwavering air, "I didn't lie- I never have."

Rudy knew what he meant. He drew closer to him, held him gently, looked him in the solemn eyes, and replied, "Son, sometimes we see things we can never explain to ourselves. I know you won't lie to me, but think it out yourself. Your mother has been in heaven for ten years, which makes it- what or whom you saw- incredulous. I wish I could believe you, but it's dinnertime, and you won't want to miss having lasagna-"

"Don't tell me you cooked-"

"I did.", Rudy scoffed, assuming that he'd succeeded in distracting his son from the illusion he witnessed in the afternoon, in vain.

Nat didn't want to cause more remorse to his father. He contemplated throughout the day and was hurt every time he felt his father's voice cracking this morning. All Nat wished was for someone to be in his shoes and see what he saw that day. Nevertheless, he went downstairs to accompany his father to the dinner table. Eventually, things renormalised, and they went to sleep to wake up to another ordinary day.

Although it was a starry night, there was constant rainfall at midnight. In the morning, Rudy went to the garage, only to discover the clogged-up wheels of his car. On the other hand, both of them were getting late for office and school, respectively. Ergo, they decided to take a bus. It seemed to be a busy day, for they had been waiting at the bus stand for a while now, and Nat turned restless.

"I think I should chicken out from going-"

"No.", Rudy cut in an avid Nat.

Meanwhile, Rudy realised that he had to buy a pen, for he should have left his, at home.

"Wait here for me. I need to buy a pen."

An already restive Nat nodded while he was thinking of ways to dodge school that day. He looked around and saw fast-paced people. However, one of them caught his eyes. He could not see her face clearly from the other side of the road, but she appeared to be his mother in all likelihood.

"Mom!" he shouted from across the street.

While Rudy was at the adjacent store, waiting for the change, he could hear Nat yelling. But what he heard had left him dumbfounded. He turned towards the bus stand to see his son trying to run across the street to reach an imaginary lady. With full pace and determination to reconcile, Nat scampered towards the other side of the road. Being ignorant of the surroundings, he was hit by a six-wheeler that appeared on the road out of nowhere. Hit severely on the right side of his body, Nat flew across the street and fell on the ground. While everything happened at the spur of the moment, Rudy blankly stared at his son, bleeding profusely and yielding- an analogous sight he had always wanted to score out.

Deathtrap

The more she ran, the darker it got. Moreover, it seemed to be a ceaseless road amidst nothing save darkness. Sarita had been running for a while- an untamed leopard was behind her. She panted and gagged but never stopped. Moreover, Sarita could see not a single soul to beckon or a shack to take cover. She was about to give in, for death was inevitable that night. Suddenly, she tripped over what appeared to be a boulder and fell on the ground. The hungry leopard, behind her, approached with decreasing pace. Its yellowish eyes were glistening with Sarita's petrified face while it grunted softly: in the next moment, it pounced on her.

Abhay woke up abruptly to see his mother, simultaneously, entering his room with coffee.

"Are you alright? Whom did you expect to open the door in the wee hours?" asked Abhay's mother, keeping the tray on the adjacent table, assuming that her presence had abruptly awakened her son.

"No- it's just that I had this weird nightmare about Sarita-"

Abhay's mother had never heard anything more unusual than this- Sarita was just a maid who had joined the service a couple of months back. He didn't even know her well- they barely talked.

"Ah! Kids of now and their weird dreams- oh, my bad- nightmares! That was ludicrously odd. Anyway, get ready for school." She left the room, parting with the ghastly air of the room. With the flow of time, when Abhay went to school and met his pals, he stopped remembering anything about the nightmare.

The daylight ceased, and it was time for Abhay to retreat. It was around 5 pm, and Sarita stayed till eight. However, when he returned home, he felt something, rather someone, missing from his sight- "Sarita!" he muttered. Momentarily, he sprinted towards the kitchen to ask her mom about her.

"Is Sarita okay- I mean, did she not turn up today or leave early-" asked an anxious Abhay.

"Oh! I was about to inform an unfortunate incident - Sarita's son died of heart attack, in the morning, owing to which she would be on leave-"

"Wh-what? A heart attack? A seven-year-old dying of a heart attack? That's-"

"-unusual? Yes, just like your nightmare you were blabbing about this morning. Now, there's no need to link the two very unusual incidents-"

"Sure, mum."

Of course, it would be foolish to link the events, but Abhay couldn't refrain from doing the same. Moreover, he questioned the uncanny coincidence. On the other hand, he also thought that what he dreamt of was Sarita's death and not his son's. After overthinking for a couple of instances, he got back to watching his favourite sitcom on the television, which helped him forget and get over his pensive thoughts.

A week had passed, and Abhay didn't have nightmares, like the one involving Sarita and the notorious leopard, until the eighth day, when he dreamt of Mrs Sinha, the widowed neighbour. She was the most generous middle-aged woman the neighbourhood had ever come across. If there was something stranger than the dream, it was the sameness of the situation- the deadly darkness, the agonist of the nightmare running as fast as one could, and the ferocious leopard. Luckily, both the times, he didn't have to see any bloodbath.

"Nightmare?" asked his mother, who was at the same spot, like every morning.

"Yes, again! The same nightmare, but this time it was-" And this time, he barred himself from identifying the victim. "- it was a mere cat. Weird, huh?"

"Indeed.", nodded a mother, whose seventeen-year-old son grossed out. This time, she wasn't fraught with anxiety but was repulsed by a dreamy Abhay. Momentarily, they heard a commotion outside. While they looked through the window, they saw a crowd circling Mrs Sinha, seated in the middle of the road. Failing to understand the scene, they went out. Eventually, one of the witnesses said, "The lady's pet was run over by a reckless car a while ago, and it yielded to a brain injury." While Abhay's mother approached a weeping Mrs Sinha to console her, Abhay stood where he was- all blank.

Unlike the previous week, Abhay couldn't get the sight of the dead chihuahua out of his mind. He tried connecting both the events and came to a rugged conclusion. His thoughts were, "Sarita was a widow, and the only person her life revolved around was his son. Again, Mrs Sinha was the same but childless. But- indeed! She loved Nancy, the chihuahua, more than anyone alive! It all fits!" Abhay was complacent but worried at the same time. While he had many questions about the scene and the victims of the nightmare, the recess bell moved his sea of thoughts- they evaporated with time.

Two weeks had passed since Nancy's unexpected death, and Abhay was glad that he didn't have to transit the nightmarish nights until two more weeks passed. Precisely a month after the previous nightmare, now it was his turn. He saw himself running, panting and gagging, and tripping over the same boulder while being chased by the wicked leopard. As soon as it pounced on him, he was brought back to reality- on his cosy bed. Everything was invariant save his mother's absence. He got down from the bed and was about to check for his mother downstairs unless he saw her lying cold on the ground floor, with a liquid spread around her that appeared to contain blood and coffee.

Happy New Year!

Perhaps, the happiest news a middle-aged homemaker could get is pregnancy: Emily was no exception. The last five-odd months have been unpleasant and anxious. However, every moment of bearing a child was worthwhile. She took every teensy precaution in taking care of herself so that things didn't go south. Moreover, she was fortunate enough to get an empathetic husband like Javier.

Javier, a thirty-year-old banker, deserved everyone's reverence. He was a philanthropist and ran an NGO to shelter needy men, women, and children outside the professional world. Moreover, a few years ago, he had helped Mrs Lopez, his forty-year-old neighbour, win a criminal case against her wicked husband. Ergo everyone, who knew him, was all praises for him and blessed the expecting mother.

The banker had forgotten to carry an umbrella, owing to which he drenched in an untimely heavy downpour while returning home. As luck would have it for a benevolent man, Javier's workplace was in the neck of the woods of his house; Emily warmly received the soggy mess with a towel and a bathrobe.

"Why don't you carry your umbrella-"

"What happened has happened. Tell me how your day was. Any pain or edginess lately?"

"Javi, it's been almost five months, and you've never failed to ask me how I am. If only every woman were blessed with a husband like you!"

"Now that's what I'd call- let's say- exaggeration! I am a man who's been raised by the most beautiful parents on earth. They're the ones who deserve to be extolled-"

"- which is what makes you more likeable, dear."

Javier sat on the couch, leisurely, wrapped in a grey bathrobe. Emily followed him and sat beside him. Momentarily, she assumed a reclining position on her beloved's lap. She looked at him with a faint smile and said,

"Javi, we haven't yet talked about naming our child."

"Okay, go ahead, Em."

"Uhm, I have drafted out a few names, just hear them- if it's a boy, then Jaime, because y'know it contains both Javier and Emily! Oh, and if it's a girl-"

"Intriguing! Jaime Sebastian. I'll try my best in raising him as a man of substance-"

"Yeah, of course, Javi, me too! And, uhm, how about Freya for a name-"

"I know it's late, but can I get a cup of cappuccino? It was such a tiresome day at the bank, and I immediately wanted to get rid of this headache."

"Well- uh- sure, honey."

A sceptical Emily went to the kitchen while Javier lay down on the couch. Before that evening, none of them brought up the topic of naming their child or even guessing its gender. While she contemplated, the pot overflowed with hot milk, which was about to burn her right palm. However, the consciousness of an expecting mother had saved the day. Post that evening; she didn't bring up the topic that constantly made Javi cut in her sentences.

Four more cheerful yet queasy months went down, and the D-day knocked at the door. The ill-timed, unfathomable labour pain had started while Javier was at the bank. However, the maid was at aid, and she managed to take her to the hospital. Later on, she informed Javier.

Doused with sweat and vexation, he rushed to the hospital in no time. However, the twilight of 30th December and the perpetual traffic restricted him from reaching the destination in time. He was late, but when he went to Emily's ward, he saw the maid seated beside her and a nurse carrying, not one but two babies, in her arms.

"Are you the father?" asked the curious nurse.

"Yes- yes!"

"Oh! Congratulations, Mr Sebastian! You have been blessed with twins! And surprisingly, one is a girl and the other is a boy! Ah, nature's beauty-"

"Indeed.", replied Javier, wearing a faint smile.

He approached the twins, had a look at them, and asked the nurse a question that startled her, "Which one's the boy?"

The weirded-out nurse handed him the boy-child. During these happenings, Emily was conscious but too tired to open her eyelids or speak. But she was all ears. And momentarily, she knew that her gemlike husband had a negative side. However, even later on, she didn't question him. Meanwhile, Javier was lulling the boy and seemed pleased while the girl was in the maid's arms.

The day ceased, and it was New Year's Eve. Emily and Javier, along with their children, returned home to embark on the remarkable journey of parenthood. They were greeted by their neighbours, who had always wished for their well-being. A mother of two, Emily, entered the house with the boy while the other child was with Javier. It was a holiday, so that Javier would be home-bound all day. Emily went upstairs with the babies to let them rest in a cute, blue-coloured pram they had bought for the child, instead, children, while Javier was in the kitchen, preparing lunch for them. The maid was on leave for a couple of days.

Javier had made themselves a scrumptious lunch. While Emily came to the dining room, she perceived an unprecedented, pensive look worn by Javier. She approached her and asked, "Is everything okay with you? Even yesterday, you behaved oddly-"

"Yeah, honey, what would happen to me- I am excellent!" scoffed a sketchy Javier.

After enjoying the lunch and Emily, breastfeeding the babies, they went to bed for a cosy afternoon nap.

Although Emily had set the alarm for seven in the evening, it somehow got set to twelve. Hours passed by, and the exhausted Emily didn't wake up until she felt her husband missing from the bed. She opened her eyes and could see nothing in the darkness of the night. However, it wasn't pitch-dark due to numerous LED lights being hung and fitted in the streets and other houses. She reached for the bed lamp and found a piece of paper. Turning on the light, she read, "Forgive me, Em.". It was Javier's handwriting, of course, but what was he sorry for?

Javier wasn't around. All these sudden events started worrying Emily. Eventually, she went towards the pram and saw the two kids sleeping profoundly. However, she felt something uncanny with one of the babies. She lifted it and sat on the floor in terror- it wasn't breathing.

Meanwhile, the clock struck twelve and the joyous screams of "Happy New Year" on the streets transcended the mournful yapping of Emily.

Vanity

It usually doesn't rain at this time of the year. However, the monsoon seemed to be definitely on its way, as the land had experienced two consecutive sad, drizzly days. The trees, on the contrary, standing firm along the road to Fred's office, were elated to perceive the moisture-laden winds from every direction.

Driving at nightfall, especially when it's accompanied by untimely and incessant rainfall, is dangerous. Despite knowing this, Fred was bent on working night shifts so that he wouldn't have to deal with the wrath of his wife, who's a teacher at a nearby primary school, and leaves home early in the morning. By the time he returns, his crabbed spouse, Amanda, would be off to school. He had been pulling all-nighters since last year without knowing the dreadful aftermath.

Fred's job at the call centre was more frustrating than Amanda's. He has always wanted to resign, but to no avail- his minimal qualifications didn't allow him to take up another job. Moreover, his feisty boss won't let him "early leaves". Nevertheless, on one fine evening, Mr Camp, wearing an atypical smirk, asked the employees to finish working before ten o'clock- "working", which comprises answering calls and calling unknown numbers.

The worst part of ill-timed monsoons is the weird frigidity they bring home- windy rainfalls, with lightning streaks, are nightmarish. When the clock struck ten, Fred had mixed feelings about going home- he was cheerful to be released earlier and anxious to return home and faced Amanda, who was probably awake. Before leaving the office, he pulled out his black umbrella and put it overhead, but the rain was too wroth not to drench him. Soaked and cold, he entered the car and started driving.

The only sound Fred could hear, besides his car skidding sporadically, was that of the raindrops pouring heavily on his car. The situation worsened when occasional flashes of lightning hindered his driving. His home was distant from his workplace; hence he tried driving as fast as he could. It usually takes forty-odd minutes for him to reach home by car, but that day, he had already spent an hour driving on, what seemed to be, a no-man's land.

While driving, something twinkled, which wasn't lightning but a fluorescent sign on his left. As he got distrait, he thought he hit something- or, someone. He stopped his car with a jounce and got out; the lengthy raindrops barred him from discovering the object. He squinted and walked forward until he felt something at his feet. Turning on a torch he always carried, he saw a girl’s body lying cold in the middle of the road. A timid man that he was, Fred stood blankly.

"Should I check her pulse- is she even alive- I shall rush her to the hospital, shan't I-"

Without thinking further, he lifted her, laid her down on the back seat, and drove her to the nearest hospital he could think of. The wicked rainfall ceased a while before they reached the destination. The posterior part of the girl's head was blood-smeared and wet with rainwater. She was still bleeding and, while Fred carried her to the hospital compound, she dripped blood along the path. Her face was unrecognisable due to a facial injury. Momentarily, she was attended to by a doctor and a couple of nurses while Fred was interrogated.

"How are you related to the patient?" asked the curious doctor.

"I'm not- see, I'm going to speak straight- it was raining cats and dogs, and I was en route to home by car, and I couldn't see anything, so I hit this girl I don't know-" replied Fred, breathlessly.

Raising his eyebrows, the doctor replied, "I see, Mr.-?"

"Fred Schilling."

"Mr Fred Schilling. I'm afraid you need to stay here till the girl regains consciousness- if she dies, you'll be charged with murder."

Fred had no reply. She sat in the general waiting room while the injured girl was taken to the ICU. Half an hour had passed, and Fred was thinking of calling Amanda- he knew his wife might divorce him for the unforeseen incident. However, he took up courage and called her.

"What is it? What do you want?"

"Am-Amanda, could you come to Green View Hospital? Now? I know it's almost midnight, but-"

"Wait- what happened? Are you alright?"

Fred was, in a way, moved to hear his wife concerned for him after numerous years. People don't change abruptly- circumstances or unforgivable events do. And Amanda was unable to forgive him for showing a devil-may-care attitude towards raising their long-lost daughter, Sonia. Fred had always been an ignorant father, but he didn't love her daughter any less than himself. But, he proved himself to be the worst at parenting when he took her girl to a fair and got detached from her amid the insane crowd. Even after searching her for months, there wasn't one clue that could lead the police to her. Post six-odd months of losing Sonia, Amanda had given in, and her overall demeanour went haywire. Through the years, she had developed a fiery ball of hatred for her delinquent husband.

"I'm fine, Amanda. You'll know once you get here-"

"Aight. I'll be there as soon as possible."

Amanda drove hastily to the said hospital. When she entered the waiting room, she could see a morose Fred, holding a pale aspect. She sat on the empty seat beside him and asked him to spill the tea. Gradually, she came to know everything and went blank in the head. Given the worst scenario- the girl's death, Fred would land in jail, and Amanda didn't want to lose anyone again. Despite exploding with rage- as Fred had thought she would- she consoled him and said, "Don't worry. Things won't go south."

Meanwhile, the police were summoned to get the details of the girl. While they did not know who the girl was, the doctors were busy attending to her. After almost an hour, one of the doctors came out of the Unit, approached Fred and Amanda, and said, "She's alive. But a serious brain injury has sent her to a coma."

Both relieved and anxious, Fred asked the doctor, "Well-uhm, that's both good and bad, but have you found anything about her?"

"Yes..." replied the doctor, optimistically, " the police confirmed that she is a twenty-two-year-old woman- oh, and she goes by the name Sonia."

Belonging to the Night

Juan's transferable job made him pack and move, from place to place, with his wife, Grace, and son, Luis. Since the beginning of time, his friends have asked him to quit the current venture and get another so that they won't have to be hypothetical vagabonds that they've been for more than a decade. However, he'd always dismiss their unanimous proposal by sticking the "high salary" note. Nevertheless, what mattered was the family being happy...and they were.

This time, the Carlos family were to shift to Valencia; moreover, it was, supposedly, the last reassignment before Juan's retirement. Hence, he decided to buy a house at the heart of the beautiful city.

Luis checked the truck for the thirteenth time and ensured that she hadn't left any of her teenager-worthy, valuable belongings in her room, in the apartment they were about to abandon.

"I'll miss my room-"

"- and this is the thirteenth time you've said it...but this is certainly the last time you're saying it!" exclaimed Juan, while cutting in Lyda's sentence.

"oh, c'mon, dad, we've lived here for more than a year, and it's quite obvious to develop feelings for this shack of a thing-" scoffed Lyda.

"- Nevertheless, let's see if you call our ultimate home shack-"

"Okay, stop, both of you- Juan, start driving...we have to reach Valencia before nightfall..." fretted a pragmatic Grace.

Noontide. Nobody, not even Juan, had thought that they'd reach the destination beforehand. Grace was content with having come before twilight so that they'd get adequate time to set up everything, and then she would also have to cook dinner for the three of them.

Time fluxed incessantly, and it seemed that the clock had struck nine o'clock in a blink. Luis and his father unpacked every stuff and kept them in the desired spots. As soon as they were done refurbishing the drawing-room, Grace called them at the dinner table. The first nights have always been dreadful for the Carlos family- an air filled with dust and newness. None of them cared to bring up any topic while dining, for they were too tired even to eat. After devouring the food clumsily, they went to bed.

Sometimes, exhaustion doesn't let us close our eyelids and sleep in peace, and it happens primarily to teenagers of Luis' age. The new house was immense; the rooms were more prominent than those in previous homes. The mattress was cosy and should have put Luis to a profound sleep, but to no avail. He was staring at the platform like it was about to collapse on him. He was used to shifting, but this was different- she couldn't explain to himself, but he couldn't deny it too.

An additional feature of the house was a terrace, covering the entire upper side of each part of the house's ceilings- it was massive! Although it was not a suitable time to go upstairs for some air, he couldn’t resist himself according to the wall clock. Moreover, as he thought, his parents were dead asleep and wouldn’t be waking up before dawn. He sprung up on the bed and left for the terrace.

It was almost midnight, yet the city wasn't asleep. The location of the three-story house was such that one could see every corner of the town, with a radius of a few kilometres. Luis had never seen something as breathtaking as this since the family's fifth shift to Bilbao. In all directions, he saw a plethora of houses, lined together, of the same height and design. What surprised him more was a human on the terrace of the adjacent house, which later appeared to be a boy.

While Luis, who didn't speak, thinking it to be a bad idea, stared at him for a few moments so that he'd notice his presence while the unknown boy was stargazing. He was about to utter the first word in the last few hours when the boy looked him in the eyes. He froze, without any idea about the next step. The boy smirked and got off the railing, to Luis' relief.

"What brings you to the terrace at this hour?" asked the stranger, out of the blue.

"Well, firstly, it's Luis, who feels uncomfortable talking to strangers, as you'd phrased, at this hour...."

"But this stranger, Sean, is your neighbour, right? And we seem to be of the same age- sixteen?"

"Observant, indeed. Well, I'm seventeen, so you got a bit mistaken-"

"Leaving that aside, you shifted here today? I saw a bunch of six-wheelers this afternoon- "

"Yes- tell me one thing, do you spend the entire day on the terrace?"

Sean scoffed and said, "Well, it depends on my mood, and me seeing you all in the afternoon was an absolute coincidence...so, nothing to worry about! Also, I'm more of a night person."

Amid the starry darkness of the midnight, Luis could see a pair of eyes glistening at him with an ineffable emotion. Slowly, when the gibbous moon shone at Sean's aspect, as brightly as it could, Luis saw a short, handsome boy whose deep and captivating voice had already talked him into liking the stranger. However, what appeared ridiculous was him wearing a blue jumper at around one o'clock.

They were exchanging glances and reciprocating through conversations, from one terrace to another. But, eventually, Sean got bored of it.

"Mind if I come over to your terrace?" asked Sean, still wearing a smirk.

"What? No, of course not! Don't you see the huge space between the two buildings? You'll trip and-"

"- die? Uh, I don't fear death. Close your eyes and count from ten to one- then open it once I tell you to."

"No way, this is too risky- besides, whence you jump, you'll wake my parents-"

"Don't worry, you can trust me."

Anxious yet calm, Luis did the same and started counting backwards. When she was at four, Sean asked him to see. There he was, standing right in front of him- a somewhat taller human being that appeared shorter, with an intriguing snigger, blonde hair, and a patchy beard. For a while, Luis gazed at him till he muttered a sarcastic "What are you looking at?". Luis came back to reality and said, "That's not important…what's more important is you answering my questions- (a), why are you wearing a jumper at midnight?- and (b), how did you jump across the gap and land here safely?"

Sean laughed hysterically at Luis' questions, which began to scare him. After all, Sean was someone he'd come across only minutes ago. He also thought that having him on the terrace, especially at that time, without her parents knowing, could be troublesome. On the contrary, their conversations or Sean's impulsive actions didn't wake anyone, which kept him out of trouble.

"So what do you do in the daytime?" asked Sean, totally out of the blue.

"Oh- uhm, you mean school or something-"

"Indeed."

"Well, due to my transient life, I wasn't that fortunate to attend one, but online degree courses do the job, really good. So, I'm usually at home, given the fact that I have a couple of friends in Bilbao and a bunch of online friends- that's that, my life is pretty boring."

"You at least have a life.", Sean whispered to himself.

"Wh-what?"

"I meant, you at least have friends to talk to...I have nobody- "

"- and who says so? We could be friends- what say, homie?"

Sean giggled at Luis' expressive way of pronouncing homie. He nodded for a "yes".

There was a water tank on the terrace, beside which both of them were seated. Each passing minute of their conversation opened an unprecedented chapter of their individual lives. Luis has mostly never had the opportunity to talk to someone his age, but now he had Sean, who wasn't a stranger anymore. Everything about Sean attracted Luis to endure the chit-chat. Although Sean seemed to be sketchy for whispering things to himself, his way of speaking and the remarkable aura about him compensated for his weird self-whispering stance.

It started getting brighter as it was time for the crack of dawn- they had successfully pulled an all-nighter! Meanwhile, Luis remembered that his father is an early bird, and if he notices him out of bed at wee hours, it won't be good for him; he didn't want to get reprimanded in the new house on "Day 1".

"I think we should return to our rooms before any of us gets scolded.", agitated Luis. With a pause, he resumed, "Well, in these four-odd hours, we've known a lot of things about ourselves."

"Well, not exactly. I got a secret- not a secret; it's reality, to be precise. But, we'll talk about it the other day. It's almost five o'clock, and I should return before the sun comes up. Okay, so goodbye, Luis, my new homie. It was a great encounter…."

"Of course- you don't know how relieved I am to get a new buddy, in person!"

While cackling at his own words, something got in Luis' right eye. He winced and tried to get the bit out with his pinky finger. It took him a couple of minutes, and by the time he could see again, Sean wasn't in sight. It was, as he thought to himself, was eerie of him. Moreover, he still had several questions for Sean to answer, including "the secret". Ergo, he decided to drop in at his house in the afternoon. Luis was tired the entire day but didn't let his parents realise it for any apparent reason. He was impatient in his room, as all he wanted was to visit Sean at around two.

It was two past fifteen, and Luis, sporadically dozing off, didn't keep track of the time. With swollen yet bright eyes, Luis emerged out of the house without informing his parents. He went to the doorstep of Sean's home, which vibrated like one of the quaint country cottages, and pressed the annoying electric bell. The door was answered by a lady, who seemed to be of his mother's age.

"Yes?" asked the lady with a faint smile.

"Good afternoon, ma'am. My family and I have shifted to the house adjacent to yours, so I, on behalf of my parents, decided to drop in!" replied Luis in the utmost cheerful way he could.

"Oh, sure, come in, young man!"

He entered the living room while his eyes were searching for his new friend; however, his eyes went on, what appeared to be, a family photo, with Sean, the lady, and a man in it. He pointed towards Sean and asked, "Your family?" The lady's eyes welled up but controlled from tearing up. With a throaty voice, she replied, "Indeed- my son and husband. They passed on two years ago, in a car crash."

Scarred for Life

Rose never seemed to be fine with me in any way- why would she? I've never blamed her, for I've done nothing but inflict excruciating pain on her, for months- pardon, for years! Since the day I was created- my creator being a splinter- I had been looked down upon by Rose's exquisite, narrow eyes, glimmering with the awful past of my unwanted creation. She was young and playful when she had me. Ever since, my juvenile mistress has tried out every way to cut me out of her life, pun intended, but in vain.

With puberty hitting hard on the girl, her hair started growing flawlessly, and she did a thing with it, what millennials call it, "bangs". It was a significant step, and a successful one, to obscure me as much as possible. Every morning, as she looked in the mirror before heading over to school, she observed me and used her great bangs against me for quite a long time. It feels like the guilt that I've borne for years is no more in existence after she created those- it makes me happy more than it does her. Since the beginning of time, Rose has been jolly and confident- her confidence skyrocketed as soon as I was not in her way to make her feel low about herself. She had befriended tons of kids at her school and in the neighbourhood- a "people's favourite".

As time slicked its way as it does, Rose was about to turn eighteen. Just before a month or two, a new boy- a foreign exchange student with prominent, charismatic features and a delightful accent- joined the same school as Rose. Moreover, he landed up as Rose's classmate.

It was a winning season of spring that matched with my mistress' vibe- it seemed like there was something besides the season, or the people around her, that had made her more vibrant than ever! Being located closer to her mind, I read it in no time- "Steve" was written all over the page! However, she was not the only young adult to have fallen for the latest student- he was, as it appeared from outside, was the ideal partner anyone could ever imagine. Rose was a part of this exceptionally talented trio that, besides him, comprised two of her best friends- Amy and Katy. While Rose was smiling to herself, she was interrupted with a pat by the two other girls.

"Who were you thinking about?" asked the other girls simultaneously.

Getting asked directly about Steve, which they weren't aware of, she replied, "I'm just taking in the, you know, air- the calming, lovely air that spring has to offer…."

"That's it? Is the air putting a smile on your face these days? Or is it the new guy in our class?" asked Amy derisively.

"What- no- I don't even know him-" stammered my mistress.

"So does no one, milady. But Katy and I noticed something very scandalous in class."

"Oh c'mon, why would I be gazing at him-" realising what she had just blurted out, Rose stopped midway.

"And the secret is out, huh!"

Rose giggled while blushing, followed by sarcastic smirking of Amy and Katy. While they were enjoying a racy conversation in front of the school gate, my seemingly master arrived- there he was, across the lane, with attributes as perfect as my mistress' eyes had ever perceived. Steve saw the girls, his classmates and approached them when he realised that one of them, especially Rose, was staring at him. He smiled, his usual luring one, at Rose and then at the rest of the trio, and headed towards the classroom.

"See? See! Steve smiled at you, Ro- you got to approach him soon, okay? Don't forget. You have too many competitions!"

"Y'know what, both of you, I think I'm gonna make a start!"

Rose's statement made all three delighted, and with the newfound joy, they went inside.

As I've already mentioned how close I am to Rose's mind, I know everything that it's up to. She wished for the first half to end, which was an unprecedented page of the book, for she'd never wanted this to happen. She was distracted, perhaps, by Steve, who happened to be as intelligent and diligent as her. While I read subtle thoughts in her mind-book, they were suddenly erased by the professor's exclamation, "Rose? I asked for an answer from you!"

"Oh, I- I don't know what it is."

"Well, someone's clearly out of focus, so why don't you, ma'am, get your ignorant self out of my class immediately?"

My mistress had never faced a similar situation, as embarrassing as this, before. Moreover, she flushed in disappointment, in Steve's presence, who was seated in the front and was not looking at her. Now that she was distraught, she walked out of the classroom. Before leaving the room, she decided to look at "the guy"- and she did- and she was glad, for he looked back with a flustering smile.

Finally, it was recess, and it had never felt like aeons for it to come. She saw Amy and Katy leaving the classroom, and they spotted her. But, behind them, was Steve, trying to scamper through the crowd, towards- her!

"So, uhm, what happened to you today, Rose? You were-"

Steve's husky voice was cut in by Rose's instant reply, "out of the world?".

"Yes, I wasn't focused enough to hear what Professor Brian had asked me to answer because-"

"- the cause is me, right? I'd been observing you for a couple of days and noticed that, well-"

"- Okay, enough with this- yes. I'd been staring at you for quite a long time- for days because, you know, I, kind of, like you-?"

"Okay, now I know. And let me tell you, I do like you too!"

Both Rose and Steve grinned at both of their confessions and shared amorous glances- and realised that they were at school. The girl was thrilled- me too. Post years of pain and self-hatred, she was finally in a happy place and not thinking about me- that being my only desire. Things were beautiful, and the air was more optimistic than ever, until Steve said, "You know what, Rose, your bangs are one of a kind- I love them!" And with this statement, my mistress and I were back to square one. I could read her mind if I wanted but didn't, for I knew what precisely the pages would read. Fun fact, she had almost forgotten about my existence, as nobody, in recent years had reminded her of me, being deep-rooted in her forehead, like an ugly parasite. If only Steve hadn't commented about them.

Hardly did a faint "yeah, of course- " turn out of her mouth when he lifted his right arm to go for the curtains that hid me. Rose's heart began sinking, and an unknown fright made her motionless- she wanted to stop and hold his arm, but she didn't- she couldn't. Eventually, he grabbed her bangs and felt something rough underneath- definitely, me. After drawing the curtains, he saw quite a lengthy, bloated, dried, reddish scar that looked scary. Steve glanced at me for a few moments and didn't say anything, which was a mistake. Rose assumed his silence to be rejected and hurried towards the washroom.

It should be noted that Amy and Katy were watching all these from a couple of meters away, and when they saw their other half running away, they thought that he had been harsh to my mistress. Enraged, they went to Steve and asked what just happened.

In utter dismay, Steve replied, "I just touched her bangs and might have-"

"Did you say anything about the scar?" asked a curious and angry Katy.

"No- no I just- I was just weirded out by that thing-"

"That thing". That awful thing that had been bugging Rose for years, but it had subsided till Steve rekindled it. Disgusted at herself and me, Rose went inside the washroom and stood in front of the mirror. She budged her bangs and looked at me- she hadn't done that for almost two years. She continued glancing, and while she did, my abiotic self grew anxious. After a while, she raised her arm, and then another, and used quite a lot of strength to rub me off. I started bleeding- surprisingly- the dried scar had never really dried up. She realised that she couldn't obliterate me, but I continued bleeding while remembering how I was created and that it was never my fault.

Against all odds

"My body hurts- we've been gliding forever!"

"Yeah, mine too. Look at us drifters- no destination, no motivation-"

To the last few words, Kit threw a hysterical laugh and remarked, "What do you need motivation for?" Kit's take somewhat vexed Kate, but he was the only strength she had, perhaps, the only motivation.

The wind howled right at their flat, sharp faces and took them places- places that were unknown and appeared to be eerie. Nightfall was on its way, making it quite challenging to see and conclude what was happening 'round them or where they were.

"Ugh, I need some rest, Kate."

"Oh, about that- you know you can do nothing about that. If only we had wings to fly voluntarily!"

They kept on gliding across lands, and the wind seemed quite uptight about not halting the process. Eventually, a shred of light began gleaming across the horizon, and, in the nick of time, the sun came up all bright and fresh. Both

Kit and Kate were mute for a while, but when they could see stuff in daylight, Kit said, "Okay, what is this place- it's not even a place- is this an ocean?"

"Think so. We've been gliding for ages now, that's that."

They were pretty above the sea level, making their way through fleecy clouds, with sunlight falling on them, either directly or down through the clouds. The wind's behaviour was quite erratic- one time, it was so forceful that it made the couple travel miles in a few moments, while in the next, it was too still even to let them glide.

"What's wrong with the wind guy today? It's being childish!" disgruntled a weary Kit.

"At least, it's not letting us dive into the ocean underneath- we're alive only because of the guy you just called a child.", rebuked Kate.

"All I want to do is reach somewhere- a land, of course, where we could rest-"

"Have some patience, Kit- we've made it this far. We're going to get somewhere worthy."

Kit wasn't satisfied with her partner's comment, so he decided to remain mute for a while.

The birds were awake by then and were flying stealthily across the waters, some of them keeping pace with Kit and Kate. Most of them were smaller compared to Kit, as he thought, so they probably won't pose any hindrance in their way. Both Kit and Kate were wearing weary faces and were seemingly bored to death. While Kate, who was gliding ahead of Kit, spotted something weird at a distance.

"Hey, Kit, do you see smoke towards the horizon?"

Kit, who had dozed off for a while, came back to his senses with a jolt and saw what he was asked to- a part of the sky was filled with dark grey smoke that appeared to be impermeable.

"Well, I think we're somewhere near a continent- they look like industrial fumes-"

"Industries, along an ocean? Kit, open your eyes, look properly-"

After scrutinising well, those indeed appeared not to be industrial fumes but seemed to be the aftermath of a deadly explosion.

"We're definitely near some land, but is it destroyed?" asked Kate worriedly.

"Can't be overruled- ugh, we were finally about to reach somewhere, and now there's an explosion there-"

Kate didn't reciprocate that but started contemplating.

The wind, this time, took a tremendous pace and took them faster than they could've ever imagined. As they were getting closer to the veil of smoke, it felt warmer and uneasy. At one point in time, they were right above the cloud of smoke, but far away for them not to perish in thin air. Momentarily, the cloud was gone, and they could see things- things that were beyond their thinking.

It was, indeed, a land- recently turned into a wasteland. Millions of stuff lying on the ground in heaps, crumbled down by a massive, artificial force; many corpses were lying on one another- men, women, and children alike- and the scenario was spread over acres and acres of lands, till the horizon.

The wind slowed down and made Kit and Kate land on one of the broken trunks of an unknown tree.

"Are we the only ones alive?"

"Indeed. Look at us, mere kites, stationed together, against all odds."

Reunion

The day could never be any worse.

Despite visiting several institutes and universities, with a worn-out file in hand, containing old degrees, Jason was refused employment everywhere he went- ill-luck.

Under the blazing sun, he crossed the road and turned homewards. On his way, it dawned upon him that it was Sunday and he should visit his wife- his deceased wife- lying beneath the earth, in a local cemetery. With a few pence in the pocket, he bought some red balloons and a bouquet of new-garnered lilies from a nearby store.

"What occasion is it anyway?" asked the curious shopkeeper.

"They're for my wife. She loves balloons...lilies too...their fragrance soothes her."

"Oh! I must say that you love your wife so dearly!"

The seventy-year-old man grinned at this sweet comment. It was already late. He's supposed to meet her sharp at noon; however, the afternoon had already struck. At this age, he scampered so rapidly that it seemed he was running for life- everyone gazed at him.

Finally, he reached there. Berta's grave was about a few meters inside, beside an old apple tree. He found it like he does every Sunday.

"Gotcha!" sighed the old man at an old, exfoliated grave. Berta Murray was engraved on the tomb along with her lifespan. It's been six years since her death, but t was just an ordinary day for Jason. He doesn't miss his wife because he articulates with her soul every day, and there's a trivial bar between them – life and death.

"I'm so sorry. I know I'm late but couldn't help it." He was about to yell out the reason but prevented himself. "Look! I've brought twenty red balloons for you, 'cause red is your favourite colour!" There was no one around but him, speaking to Berta's soul. He tied the balloons to the neighbouring tree, which shaded the grave. "I feel so bored every day…Without you, a day seems like millions of years!" He laughed cheerlessly. "On the other hand, I remain anxious about Simon. He hardly calls me…."

Simon Murray is their second son. Their first, named Mark, died in a car crash at the early age of twenty. Since then, they have pampered him, and the aftermath was appalling. He turned out to be rotten at heart. As Simon grew up, he began earning fame and reverence through fashion designing and, thus, made much cash. Regrettably, he didn't care to look after his parents. Ergo bought a mansion in California and, abandoning them, shifted there with his wife and daughter. (Berta was crestfallen when she came to know about Simon's plan of deserting her and Jason.) Alternatively, Jason was a retired professor with lesser cash in hand. However, he and Berta managed to live without Simon. Jason's giving and considerate, with a heart as soft as a cotton ball. With whatever money he had, he used it well. On one fine day, as Jason was back home after buying some fruits and vegetables, he saw his wife lying cold on the floor. He rushed to a nearby hospital. It was a day before Christmas eve, and most of the doctors were on a week's holiday. However, one of them turned up and took charge of the patient.

After half an hour, she was announced dead owing to a heart attack. Such an atrocious statement made Jason’s face pale. He sat on the floor but didn't weep. The doctor could not make out what was going on in Jason's mind. So, he kept his hands on his shoulders and helped him get up. " I'm sorry, sir.", said the doctor furtively. "It's time to bury her and inform your relatives about her demise. Do you have any…" "Son. His name's Simon. But I guess he won't come." said Jason with grief. "But you should at least let him know. After all, she is his mother!" said the doctor profoundly. Jason called him. At the sixth time, he answered his call but retorted him for disturbing him in a business meeting.

Jason was pained at his disrespectful demeanour; he had no one to share his feelings with.

Most of his relatives were dead, leaving his cousin brother, who was not even in the city. That day, he was alone in the graveyard, with the lifeless body of his soulmate and some keepers who helped him bury her.

Several mirthful memories flashed in Jason's mind. He looked up at the sky and then at the tomb. Touching it, he felt Berta's quintessence. He kept the bouquet at one end of the tomb and went away. He wanted to say many things to her, but his head was about to burst due to a headache. Moreover, the sweltering hot day made the exhausted man feel perturbed. He was sweating more than ever; he felt sick and tried to find a seat nearby, but in vain. A few meters ahead, his body gave in, and he sat on the ground, on his knees. Momentarily, his heart started aching, an ache that would undoubtedly end his state of *saudade*and reunite him with his old love, and it did.

www.ingramcontent.com/pod-product-compliance
Lightning Source LLC
LaVergne TN
LVHW050424160726
843469LV00041B/1221